Marshmallow Kisses

Linda Crotta Brennan
Illustrated by Mari Takabayashi

Houghton Mifflin Company Boston 2000

The text of this book is set in 22-point Leawood.
The illustrations are watercolor.

Library of Congress Cataloging-in-Publication Data
Brennan, Linda Crotta.
Marshmallow kisses / by Linda Crotta Brennan ; illustrated by Mari Takabayashi.
p.   cm.
Summary: Children enjoy a variety of activities during a summer day.
ISBN 0-395-73872-5
[1. Summer—Fiction. 2. Stories in rhyme.] I. Takabayashi, Mari, 1960–   ill. II. Title.
PZ8.3.B7455Mar   2000   [E]—dc21   99-36271   CIP

Manufactured in the United States of America
WOZ 10 9 8 7 6 5 4 3 2 1

For my daughters, Lisa, Diana, and
Patricia, who shared their joy in summer
days with marshmallow kisses.
—L.C.B.

For my Aunt Sadako.
—M.T.

Sun sings.
Wings fan.

Swing on porch

With toast and jam.

Paint a picture
On the stair.

Grass tickles

Feet bare.

Pail and shovel,
Pat and bake,
Dry sand icing
On wet sand cake.

Sandwich picnic

Under trees.

Hang blankets
For teepees.

Slide in pool.
Splash feet.
Fill pitchers.
Sail fleet.

Lay towels

In the sun.

Dragonflies cruise.
Bumblebees hum.

Hungry children

Slam screens.

Buttered corn.
Snapped beans.

Neighbors visit

Into the night.

Marshmallow kisses

By firefly light.